Harold's Fairy Tale

to the
enchanted
garden

*Further Adventures with
the Purple Crayon*

Harold's
Fairy Tale

*by
Crockett
Johnson*

📖 HarperCollins*Publishers*

Copyright © 1956 by Crockett Johnson
Copyright renewed 1984 by Ruth Krauss
All rights reserved. Printed in Mexico.
Library of Congress Catalog Card Number 56-8147
ISBN 0-06-022976-4 (lib. bdg.) — ISBN 0-06-443347-1 (pbk.)

One evening Harold got out of bed, took his

purple crayon and the moon along, and went

for a walk in an enchanted garden.

Nothing grew in it. If he hadn't known it
was an enchanted garden, Harold scarcely
would have called it a garden at all.

To find out what the trouble was, Harold
decided to ask the king.

Kings live in large castles. Harold had to make sure the castle was big enough to be the king's.

He didn't want to waste time talking to any princes or earls, or dukes.

This was a king's castle all right. It had
tall towers and a big draw-gate to keep out
people the king didn't want to see.

But when the draw-gate was drawn closed

it kept Harold out too.

Harold shouted for the king to come down
and let him in. But the gate didn't open.

He walked along the edge of the enchanted
garden beside the smooth wall of the castle
—until he thought of his purple crayon.

A person smaller than a very small mouse

would be able to get in.

Without even bending, he walked into a very small mousehole.

He walked through the mousehole into
the castle. He invited the mouse in too,
but the mouse preferred to stay outside.

As he gazed around inside the big castle

Harold felt very tiny.

And a king might not pay much attention

to anybody who was smaller than a mouse.

So Harold used his purple crayon again.

He made sure he was as tall as four and a half steps of stairs, his usual height.

Then he climbed up the stairs, looking for the king.

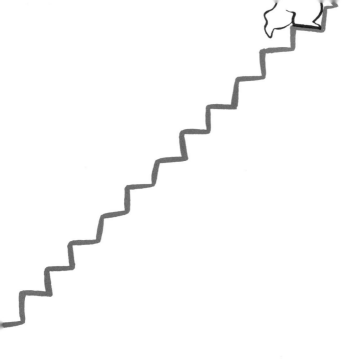

He went up and up and up, until he got so tired he couldn't climb another step.

Luckily there were no more steps. He had
reached the top.

He still couldn't find the king. But he remembered kings sat on thrones.

The king's throne looked very comfortable.
Harold thought the king wouldn't mind if
he rested a few minutes.

He sat on the throne, wondering what it was like to be a king and wear a crown.

He tried it, with the king's crown.

It was all right for a while. But the
crown began to feel heavy.

So Harold put it on the king's head.

As he thanked the king for the loan of
the crown, he noticed the king looked
sad—no doubt because of the garden.

He asked the king if the trouble was due
to a witch or a giant. The king couldn't
say which. He looked sad and helpless.

Evidently the giant or witch—if the king

couldn't tell which it was—was invisible.

But Harold told the king not to worry.

He set off to find the invisible witch or
giant, brandishing his purple crayon. And
—accidently—it made a hole in the wall.

The accident embarrassed Harold. But the hole was the handiest way out of the castle and he climbed through it.

When he looked down from the other side
of the hole, he realized he had forgotten
how high up he was.

He needed something tall to climb down
on, something as tall as a steeple.

To fill the hole in the castle, Harold put
a handsome and useful clock in it. He was
surprised to see how late it was.

He slid down the steeple, to find the invisible witch or giant right away.

It wasn't a steeple. It was a pointed hat.

It was a GIANT WITCH.

The purple crayon made it plain—it was
an invisible giant witch. Well, no wonder
nothing grew in the enchanted garden.

How could anything grow, Harold said
to himself, with a giant witch tramping
around with big feet.

Now that he saw what the trouble was, all Harold had to do was drive the witch out of the enchanted garden.

Mosquitoes. Mosquitoes, Harold knew, will drive anybody out of a garden.

The mosquitoes drove out the witch. They also were driving Harold out of the garden.

He had to make smoke to get rid of the
mosquitoes.

And he had once heard somebody say that
where there's smoke there must be fire.

To put out the fire, he first thought of fire engines. But he decided to make it rain. Rain was easier.

The rain soaked everything—Harold too.

But, he said, it's good for the flowers.

He was right. Soon there were flowers.

Beautiful flowers popped up all over the
enchanted garden, more than Harold was
able to count, all in gorgeous bloom.

Harold thought how delighted and happy
the king would be when he looked out
from the castle in the morning.

And then, amazingly, the last flower
turned out to be not a flower at all—
but a lovely fairy.

She held out her magic wand as fairies
always do when they're giving somebody
wishes that will come true.

Harold couldn't think of a thing to wish for. But, to be polite, he took one wish and told the fairy he'd use it later.

Besides, Harold thought, as he started on his long walk home, a wish might come in handy sometime.

After all the excitement he suddenly felt
tired. And he stopped to rest awhile.

He sat on a small rug because the ground
was still somewhat damp from the rain.
And he wished—

He wished the rug was a flying carpet.

At once Harold felt it rise in the air.

It flew fast and high.

But when it went so fast it left the moon
behind, Harold realized he didn't know how
to stop the carpet, or even slow it down.

He wished he'd taken two wishes from the
fairy, so he could wish the flying carpet
would land.

But he did have his purple crayon.

He landed the flying carpet in his living
room, right behind the high-backed chair
his mother sat in, knitting.

And he asked her to read him a story

before he went back to bed.